THE FINGER-EATER

Long ago, in the cold lands of the North, there lived a troll named Ulf, who had a very bad habit – he liked to eat fingers!

Dick King-Smith used to be a farmer and is now one of the world's favourite children's book authors. Winner of the Guardian Fiction Award for *The Sheep-pig* (filmed as *Babe*), he was named Children's Book Author of the Year in 1991 and won the 1995 Children's Book Award for *Harriet's Hare*. His titles for Walker include *Puppy Love*, *Dick King-Smith's Animal Friends*, *Lady Lollipop* and the popular Sophie series.

Books by the same author

Lady Lollipop
Sophie Hits Six
Sophie in the Saddle
Sophie Is Seven
Sophie's Lucky
Sophie's Snail
Sophie's Tom

DICK KING-SMITH

THE FINGER EATER

Illustrations by Arthur Robins

WALKER BOOKS
AND SUBSIDIARIES
LONDON • BOSTON • SYDNEY

For Gareth
A.R.

First published 1992 by
Walker Books Ltd, 87 Vauxhall Walk
London SE11 5HJ

This edition published 2001

2 4 6 8 10 9 7 5 3 1

Text © 1992 Fox Busters Ltd
Illustrations © 1992, 2001 Arthur Robins

The right of Dick King-Smith to be identified as author of this
work has been asserted by him in accordance with the
Copyright, Designs and Patents Act 1988

This book has been typeset in Garamond

Printed and bound in Great Britain by The Guernsey Press Co. Ltd

British Library Cataloguing in Publication Data:
a catalogue record for this book is
available from the British Library

ISBN 0-7445-8269-5

Contents

CHAPTER 1

Long long ago, in the cold lands
of the North, there lived a most
unusual troll.

Like all the hill-folk (so called because they usually made their homes in holes in the hills) he was hump-backed and bow-legged, with a frog-face and bat-ears and razor-sharp teeth.

But he grew up (though, like all other trolls, not very tall) with an extremely bad habit –

he liked to eat fingers!

Ulf (for that was his name) always went about this in the same way.

Whenever he spied someone walking alone on the hills, he would come up, smiling broadly, and hold out a hand, and say politely:

"How do you do?"

Now trolls are usually rude and
extremely grumpy and don't care
how anyone does, so the person
would be pleasantly surprised at
meeting such a jolly one, and
would hold out his or her
hand to shake Ulf's.

Then Ulf would take it and, quick as a flash, bite off a finger with his razor-sharp teeth and run away as fast as his bow-legs would carry him, chewing like mad and grinning all over his frog-face.

Strangers visiting those parts were amazed to see how many men, women and children were lacking a finger on their right hands, especially children, because their fingers were more tender and much sought after by Ulf.

Nobody lacked more than one finger, because even small children weren't foolish enough to shake hands if they met Ulf a second time, but ran away with them deep in their pockets.

It was usually the index finger
that Ulf nipped off because it was
the easiest to get at, so that many
children grew up pointing with a
middle finger…

and holding a pencil between
middle and third…

but sometimes Ulf went for the little one: thumbs, for some reason, he did not seem to fancy.

Strangely, the people of those lands were tolerant and long-suffering and seemed to put up with Ulf's bad habit.

"What can't be cured must be endured," they would say, and since they considered it was no use crying over spilt milk, they wasted no tears over lost fingers but got on with their lives with only seven.

CHAPTER 2

Who knows how long Ulf the troll
might have continued in his wicked
ways if it had not been for a little
girl named Gudrun.

Gudrun was the only child of a reindeer farmer. She had golden hair which she wore in a long plait, and eyes the colour of cornflowers.

Indeed she was as pretty as a picture, looking as though reindeer butter wouldn't melt in her mouth.

She was also a sensible child, who paid attention to what her parents told her.

One evening, as they all sat round the fire outside their tent, Gudrun's mother said to her:

Remember, you must never shake hands with a troll.

She stirred the cooking-pot that
was suspended above the flames.
The hand that held the ladle had no
little finger.

With his right hand, on which
the index finger was missing,
Gudrun's father picked
up a stick to put
on the fire.

"But why," said Gudrun, "didn't either of you do that?"

"When we were both children," said her mother, "we didn't know about the Finger-eater."

"We were among the first in this district," said her father, "to lose a finger. But now everybody knows."

"Why don't all the mothers and fathers warn their children then?" said Gudrun.

"They do," said her mother, "but sometimes the children don't listen, or they just forget. Mind you remember."

Gudrun thought deeply about
this while she was out on the hills,
helping her father herd his reindeer
as they grazed their way across
the slopes.

It's all very well, she thought, to tell children not to get their fingers eaten, but someone ought to tell that troll not to eat them. Eating people's fingers is wrong.

He should be stopped.

And being not only a very pretty
but also a very resolute child, she
resolved that she would stop the
Finger-eater. But how?

"Father," she said as she sat
milking one of the reindeer,
"how big is a troll?"

"No taller than you, Gudrun," her father said, "but much much stronger."

"Have you ever met one?"

For answer her father held up
his right hand.

"Oh yes," said Gudrun. "But since then, I mean?"

"No," said her father, "but I have quite often seen the hill-folk, just for a moment. Then they scuttle down their holes, for they are all shy of people. Except Ulf the Finger-eater."

"You have never seen him again?"

"No, and nor will you, I hope."

But not long after, Gudrun did.

Even in those bleak Northern lands
there are days in the short summer
which are bright and warm and
flower-filled, and on such a morning

Gudrun's father handed her a flask.
It was made of reindeer skin, was
this flask, and it was stopped with a
cork made out of reindeer
horn, and it was
filled with fresh,
rich reindeer
milk.

"Be a good girl and take this to your mother," her father said, for the herd's grazing grounds were not far from the family tent, and it did not occur to him that she might come to any harm.

Gudrun set off across the hill, carrying the flask in her right hand. Before she had gone far she saw, in a steep bank, a large hole.

Could that be the home of one of the hill-folk? she thought, and no sooner had she thought it than out of the hole came a hump-backed, bow-legged figure with a frog-face and bat-ears.

Straight towards her he came, his mouth agape in a friendly smile, his hand outstretched. "How do you do?" he said politely.

The Finger-eater! thought Gudrun and she remembered her parents' advice to put her hands in her pockets and run. But I won't, she said to herself bravely, for now may be my only chance to make the Finger-eater see how wrong it is to eat fingers. So she stood her ground.

"I'm sorry," she said, "but I cannot shake your hand because I'm holding this flask of milk."

"You could always hold it with your other hand," said Ulf, for it was he.

"I could," said Gudrun, "but I
won't. I've heard of you, you see.
You are Ulf the Finger-eater."

"Well, well," said Ulf, passing his
tongue across his razor-sharp teeth,
"and what is your name, little girl?"

"It's Gudrun. Now let me tell you something, Ulf," she said. "Eating fingers is wrong."

A clever little miss, thought Ulf. How can I trick her? He sat down on a nearby tree-stump, and crossed one bow-leg over the other, looking serious and thoughtful.

"You're right, Gudrun," he said.
"I'm wrong to eat people's fingers,
I see that now. But at least give me
a drink of milk."

And when she holds out the
flask, he thought, I'll soon have one
of those lovely little pink sausages!

"Not on your life," said Gudrun. "Thanks to you, both my mother and my father are short of a finger."

"How time flies!" said Ulf. "That must have been when I was a very young troll. I've probably had a hundred fingers since then."

"Well, you're not having a hundred and one," said Gudrun, "but on second thoughts I'll give you that drink," and pulling out the cork, she jerked the flask so that the milk shot out straight into Ulf's frog-face, and as he stood gasping, she dashed away.

CHAPTER 4

Gudrun did not tell her parents
of her meeting with Ulf. She simply
said she had tripped, the cork had
come out of the flask, and the milk
had all spilled (a white lie, she
told herself).

47

But she continued to think long and hard about the Finger-eater. Somehow or other he must be made to give up his horrid habit.

Then one day Gudrun had a sudden, brilliant idea.

She was sitting outside the family tent, playing with a reindeer antler. This was the time of year when all the reindeer (for the cows are horned as well as the bulls) shed their antlers before growing fresh ones, and they were lying about everywhere. Hard as iron they were, and many of them were of the strangest shapes, for reindeer antlers are very large and many-pointed, those of some of the bulls curving right round and down until they almost meet the animals' faces.

The single antler that Gudrun held was quite a small one, probably from a young beast, but at its tip it had an odd shape, something like a human hand. It had at its end a flat surface resembling the palm of a hand and from this surface five points protruded. Just like four fingers and a thumb, thought Gudrun, and that was when the idea hit her.

That afternoon Ulf emerged from his hole to see Gudrun approaching, her long blonde plait swinging as she walked, her cornflower-blue eyes sparkling, her right hand, much to the troll's surprise, already outstretched in greeting. Admittedly she was wearing a large pair of reindeer hide gloves, but those won't save her, thought Ulf.

He advanced to meet her.

"Hello, Ulf," said Gudrun brightly.
"I've come to say I'm sorry for
throwing the milk at you. Will you
shake hands and then we can be
friends?"

Stupid child, thought Ulf. She's asking for it. This time I won't just have one finger, I'll have all four, and he grabbed Gudrun's right hand and shoved it into his frog-mouth and bit it as hard as he could.

Then Ulf's great cry of agony echoed and rang from the circling hills, as his razor- sharp teeth broke and smashed and shattered, every one.

And Gudrun drew off the mangled glove that had concealed the antler, its stem thrust up the sleeve of her blouse, and revealed that bony five-pointed end that had looked so like a hand.

"Hard luck, Ulf," she said. "You bit off more than you could chew."

"Oh! Oh!" moaned the Finger-eater. "My teeth! My teeth! Every single one is loose in my head! Oh, it is agony! Help me! Help me!"

"I will," said Gudrun, and she took from the pocket of her skirt a pair of stout pliers, a useful tool with which her father was wont to draw stones that had lodged deep between the great splay hooves of his reindeer.

"Open wide, Ulf," she said, "and I'll make you a much better troll."

Then with the pliers she pulled out the teeth of the Finger-eater, one by one, till none were left.

CHAPTER 5

Even after that, Ulf could not
easily rid himself of his bad habit.

Once his mouth was no longer sore, he still tried several times to live up to his name, but thanks to Gudrun, he could not. For though the reindeer can grow new antlers, hill-folk cannot grow new teeth, and those few people whose hands he caught only giggled at the harmless pressure of his toothless gums upon their fingers and told him not to be such a silly old troll.

So that before long Ulf fell into a
terrible sulk, and disappeared down
his hole in the hill, and was never
seen again.

And even today, if you travel in the cold old North and stay amongst the reindeer people, you may hear the tale of the troll named Ulf and the girl called Gudrun, and how she and she alone put paid to the wicked ways of the Finger-eater.

More ~~SPRINTERS~~ for you to enjoy!

- *Little Stupendo Flies High* Jon Blake — 0-7445-5970-7
- *Captain Abdul's Pirate School* Colin McNaughton — 0-7445-5242-7
- *The Ghost in Annie's Room* Philippa Pearce — 0-7445-5993-6
- *Molly and the Beanstalk* Pippa Goodhart — 0-7445-5981-2
- *Taking the Cat's Way Home* Jan Mark — 0-7445-8268-7
- *The Finger-eater* Dick King-Smith — 0-7445-8269-5
- *Care of Henry* Anne Fine — 0-7445-8270-9
- *The Impossible Parents Go Green* Brian Patten — 0-7445-7881-7
- *Flora's Fantastic Revenge* Nick Warburton — 0-7445-7898-1
- *Jolly Roger* Colin McNaughton — 0-7445-8293-8
- *The Haunting of Pip Parker* Anne Fine — 0-7445-8294-6
- *Tarquin the Wonder Horse* June Crebbin — 0-7445-7882-5

All at £3.99